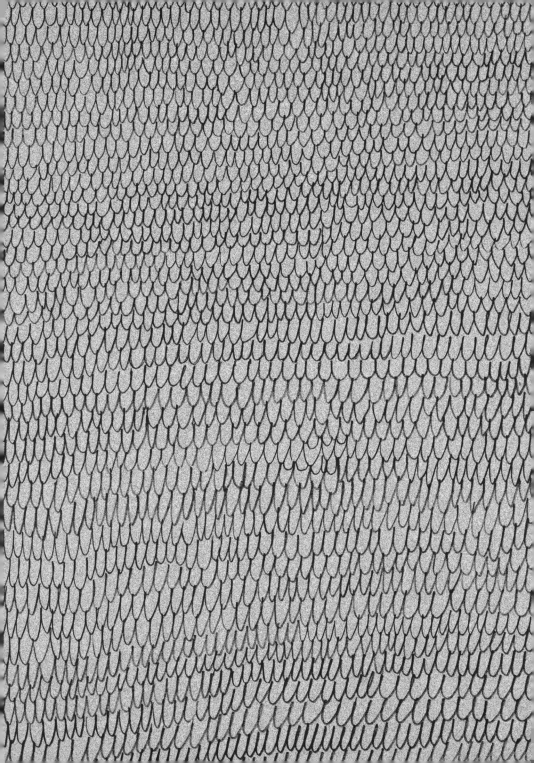

I DIDN'T DO MY HOMEWORK BECAUSE...

Georgetown Elementary School
Indian Prairie School District
Aurora, Illinois

To Valentino and Ben
—Davide

For Milo
—Benjamin

Text copyright © 2014 by Davide Cali.
Illustrations copyright © 2014 by Benjamin Chaud.

Library-of-Congress Cataloging-in-Publication Data Available.

ISBN 978-1-4521-2551-0

Manufactured in China.

Book design by Amy Yu Gray.
Typeset in 1820 Modern.

10 9 8 7 6 5 4 3 2

Chronicle Books LLC
680 Second Street, San Francisco, California 94107

Chronicle Books—we see things differently. Become part of our community at www.chroniclekids.com.

I DIDN'T DO MY HOMEWORK BECAUSE...

Davide Cali   Benjamin Chaud

chronicle books · san francisco

"So, why didn't you do your homework?"

I didn't do my homework because...

An airplane full of monkeys landed in our yard.

A rebellious robot destroyed our house.

Elves hid all of my pencils.

I was abducted by a UFO.

Just when I started to do my homework,
we were attacked by Vikings.

Giant lizards invaded my neighborhood.

Some cough medicine that my doctor prescribed
had a strange effect on me.

I had to help my uncle build a high-tech do-my-homework-for-me machine, but when we finally finished, it didn't work.

My dog was swallowed up by *another* dog,
so I spent the afternoon at the vet.

I was at my cat's funeral.

Some escaped convicts from the local jail hid in
my bedroom and wouldn't come out.

My uncle was challenged to a duel by a neighbor.

My grandpa and his band were making
too much noise, and I couldn't concentrate.

We ran out of firewood, so I sacrificed
my workbooks to stay warm.

We found a lost penguin, so we took
him to the North Pole—

"But penguins
live at the
South Pole!"

Exactly! When we realized our mistake, we had to
come back and take him to the *other* Pole . . .

My brother and I were kidnapped by a circus.

My family discovered oil in our backyard.

I gave my pencils to Robin Hood.

A famous director asked to use
my bedroom to shoot his new movie.

Some strange birds made a nest on our roof.

We had a problem with carnivorous plants.

Our roof suddenly disappeared.

The neighbors asked if we could help them
look for their armadillos.

My sister's rabbit chewed up
all of my pencils and workbooks.

My brother had his little problem again.

A tornado swept up all of my books.

So . . . why don't you believe me?

Giant lizards never invaded my neighborhood.
Giant lizards never invaded my neighborhood.
Giant lizards never invaded my neighborhood.
Giant lizards never invaded my neighborhood.
Giant lizards never invaded my neighborhood.
Giant lizards never invaded my neighborhood.
Giant lizards never invaded my neighborhood.
Giant lizards never invaded my neighborhood.

- The End -

Davide Cali is an author, illustrator, and cartoonist who has published more than 40 books, including *I Can't Wait, The Bear with the Sword, The Enemy, What is This Thing Called Love,* and *A Dad Who Measures Up.* He lives in Paris, France.

Benjamin Chaud has illustrated more than 60 books. He is the author and illustrator of *The Bear's Song,* and he is the illustrator of the Pomelo series. He lives in Die, France.

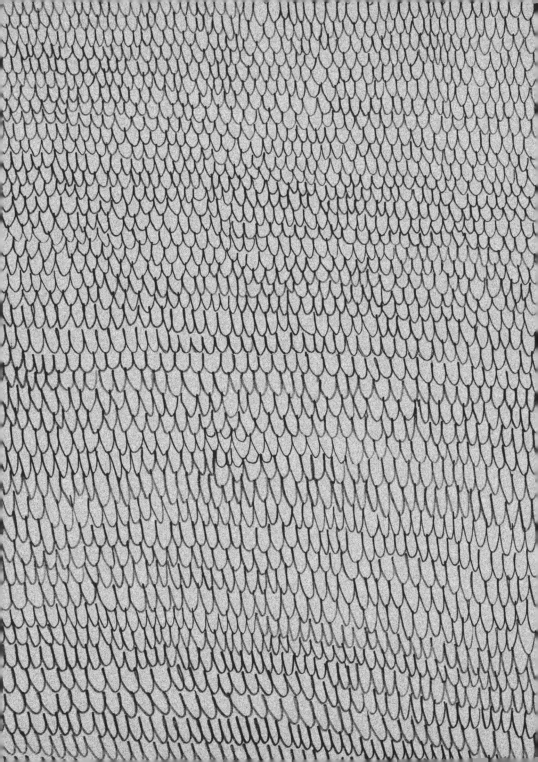

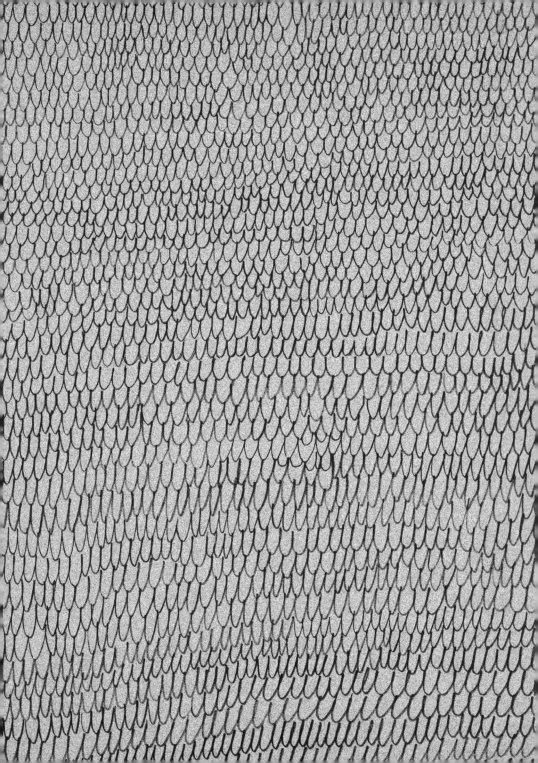